PINKY and REX
and the Bully

ATHENEUM BOOKS BY JAMES HOWE

Teddy Bear's Scrapbook
(with Deborah Howe)
A Night without Stars
Morgan's Zoo
There's a Monster under My Bed
There's a Dragon in My Sleeping Bag

BUNNICULA SERIES
Bunnicula
(with Deborah Howe)
Howliday Inn
The Celery Stalks at Midnight
Nighty-Nightmare
Return to Howliday Inn

SEBASTIAN BARTH MYSTERIES
What Eric Knew
Stage Fright
Eat Your Poison, Dear
Dew Drop Dead

PINKY AND REX SERIES
Pinky and Rex
Pinky and Rex Get Married
Pinky and Rex and the Spelling Bee
Pinky and Rex and the Mean Old Witch
Pinky and Rex Go to Camp
Pinky and Rex and the New Baby
Pinky and Rex and the Double-Dad Weekend
Pinky and Rex and the Bully

PINKY and REX
and the Bully

by James Howe
illustrated by Melissa Sweet

READY-TO-READ

ATHENEUM BOOKS FOR YOUNG READERS

Atheneum Books for Young Readers
An imprint of Simon & Schuster Children's Publishing Division
1230 Avenue of the Americas
New York, New York 10020

READY-TO-READ is a registered trademark of Simon & Schuster, Inc.

Book design by Michael Nelson

The text of this book is set in Utopia.
The illustrations are rendered in watercolor.

First edition

Printed in Hong Kong by South China Printing Company (1988) Ltd.

10   9   8   7   6   5   4   3

Library of Congress Cataloging-in-Publication Data

Howe, James, 1946–
Pinky and Rex and the bully / by James Howe; illustrated by Melissa
Sweet.—1st ed.
p. cm.
Summary: Pinky learns the importance of identity as he defends his favorite
color, pink, and his friendship with a girl, Rex, from the neighborhood bully.
ISBN 0-689-80021-5 (HC)
[1. Identity—Fiction. 2. Bullies—Fiction. 3. Friendship—Fiction.] I. Sweet,
Melissa, ill. II. Title.
PZ7.H83727Pie 1996
[E]—dc20
95-22006

To my niece, Jordana
—J. H.

To Max and Nina
—M. S.

Contents

Chapter 1
"Sissy!"

"You're a sissy, Pinky!" the boy shouted. "Get up and fight."

Pinky lay on the sidewalk where the third-grader had knocked him off his bike. His cheeks were fever-hot.

"Pinky is a gir-rl! Pinky is a gir-rl!" the older boy chanted.

"I am not," Pinky said.

The boy kicked at Pinky. "Get up, sissy, or I'll tell everybody in school tomorrow that you're a girl. Anyway, nobody but a girl would ride a pink bike—or have a name like Pinky!"

Pinky's heart pounded so hard he could feel it in his throat. Why couldn't Kevin just go away? Suddenly, he heard a door open and someone running in his direction.

"Stop that! You leave him alone!" a voice called out. Pinky recognized it as Mrs. Morgan's. Now his cheeks really burned. It was embarrassing enough to be bullied, but to be saved by an old woman made it even worse.

"It's okay, Mrs. Morgan," Pinky said, scrambling to his feet. "I . . . I just fell off my bike."

"I was trying to help him up," Kevin lied. He pretended to pat Pinky on the shoulder, but pinched him hard instead.

3

"I know what you did," Mrs. Morgan said, pushing Kevin's hand away. "I saw the whole thing. Now you get out of here before I call your parents." 5

Kevin snickered, jumped on his bike, and rode off. When he reached the end of the block, he turned back and shouted, "Sissy!"

Mrs. Morgan didn't seem to notice. "I just made lemonade," she said. "Would you like some?"

Pinky would have liked to run across the street to his own house, bury his head in his pillow, and sleep until tomorrow. But seeing as how Mrs. Morgan had just saved his life, he couldn't say no.

"Okay," he mumbled.

"Good," said Mrs. Morgan. "We'll sit out on the back porch and you'll tell me what this was all about."

Pinky groaned. 6

Chapter 2
Cookies and Lemonade

Mrs. Morgan gave Pinky cookies with his lemonade.

"You know, I hadn't baked cookies for years until you and your father made some for me," she told him. "I'd forgotten how much better they are than the store-bought kind."

"Yes, ma'am," Pinky said. They looked like good cookies, but he had no interest in eating them.

Mrs. Morgan nodded toward a large bush blooming in her backyard. "Did you ever see such an explosion of pink?" she asked. "Why, that's your favorite color, isn't it?"

Pinky blushed. His favorite color was what had gotten him into trouble with the bully. "Yes, ma'am," he answered.

"And that's how you got your nickname. You know, I don't remember your real name. I've been living across the street from you since before you were born and all I think to call you is Pinky."

"William," Pinky muttered.

9

"William," Mrs. Morgan echoed. "That's right." She took a sip of her lemonade and stared for a long time at the flowering bush. /o

"I was just thinking," Mrs. Morgan said, almost as if Pinky weren't there, "that I should paint that bush."

"Don't you like it the color it is?" Pinky asked.

Mrs. Morgan burst into laughter. "No, no, I mean I should paint a picture of it. I used to paint pictures. A long time ago."

Before she could go on, someone shouted, "Pinky!" It was Rex, waving from her driveway next door.

"Join us for cookies and lemonade,"
Mrs. Morgan called out. Rex came
running. Pinky wished his friend hadn't
seen him there. He didn't want her to
find out about Kevin pushing him off
his bike.

Luckily, the subject didn't come up. Rex was full of news about her baby brother Matthew. She talked and talked and never noticed that Pinky wasn't eating his cookies nor that Mrs. Morgan was lost in thoughts of her own. 12

Chapter 3
Recess

At recess the next day, Kevin's foot stopped the soccer ball Pinky was chasing. Pinky grabbed for it, but Kevin grabbed it first.

"How come you're always playing with girls?" Kevin asked, wrapping his arms around the ball. Pinky glanced over his shoulder at Rex.

"She's my friend," Pinky said.

Kevin laughed, which brought two other boys to his side. "This little squirt plays with girls," he told the new arrivals. "That's because he's a girl, too. Know what his name is?"

The boys looked as if they weren't sure whether to laugh or act tough.

They watched Kevin for a sign.

Kevin pursed his lips. "Pinky," he said, in a mocking way. He started to laugh. The other boys' faces relaxed as they started laughing, too.

Just then, Pinky's friend Anthony came over. "Give him back his ball," Anthony said.

"Ooo," crooned one of the boys. "Second-graders. I'm so scared."

"Yeah, well, being in third grade doesn't make you anybody," Anthony said, punching the ball hard and knocking it out of Kevin's arms.

Kevin went for it but Anthony was faster. "Come on, Pinky," Anthony said, "let's go."

Kevin started after them, then changed his mind. "Hey, kid, watch out who you play with," he shouted. "You might turn into a girl, too!"

Anthony scowled. "What's he talking about?" he asked Pinky.

Pinky shrugged. "Beats me," he said. But inside he wondered if Kevin was right. Maybe he *was* a girl.

Chapter 4
Billy

18

That night after dinner, Pinky was helping his father clean up. "Is it bad that I like pink?" he asked.

"Of course not," his father said. "Pink has always been your favorite color."

"Yeah, but now that I'm seven maybe I should like a different color."

"What does being seven have to do with it?"

Pinky put down his dish towel and slumped into a chair. Finally, he said, "Maybe you shouldn't call me Pinky anymore."

"When you were little, we called you Billy," his father said.

Pinky thought for a long time. Then he said, "From now on, I'm Billy."

Later, in his room, Pinky looked at all his stuffed animals. Every one of them had pink on it somewhere. He could just imagine what Kevin would say about them. He picked up his favorite, Pretzel the pig.

"Hi, Pretzel," he said. "I'm Billy now." The name felt funny in his mouth. "I guess I have to make some other changes, too. I just want you to know that no matter what happens, you'll always be my friend." 2/

"I heard you and Daddy talking before." z z

Pinky turned as his little sister Amanda came into his room and flopped down on the bed. "Well, I'm not going to call you Billy."

"You have to because that's my name from now on," he told her.

Amanda shrugged. "Okay, but then you have to give me your animals."

"Why?"

"Because if you're not going to be called Pinky anymore, then you can't like pink anymore. And if you don't like pink anymore, then you can't have these animals anymore."

Pinky thought about what his sister said. Then he gave her every one of his stuffed animals.

That night, he woke up several times. He looked around his empty room and wondered where he was.

Chapter 5
Hard Choices

24

The next day was Saturday.
Pinky didn't want to get up. He had
something very hard to do that morning
— maybe the hardest thing he would
ever have to do in his whole life. After
he heard Amanda go downstairs, he
sneaked into her bedroom.

"Hi, Pretzel," he whispered. "Did you miss me?"

He made Pretzel's head nod yes.

"I'm supposed to play with Rex today," he told his friend with the curly tail, "but I have to tell her I can't play with her anymore. Why? Because she's a girl, Pretzel, don't you understand?" 25

He made Pretzel's head move from side to side.

"That's because you're a pig. If you were a boy like me, you'd know that you're not supposed to be friends with girls. I mean, it's okay when you're a little kid, but not when you're seven."

Pretzel looked at Pinky with blank button eyes.

It was almost noon by the time Pinky was dressed and out of the house. Standing at the end of Rex's sidewalk, he tried to figure out the words he would say to her. None of them seemed right.

"Why, hello there, Pinky," he heard Mrs. Morgan call out. She was sitting on her front porch, looking through her mail.

"My name is Billy now," he told her.

"What's that?"

Pinky went to Mrs. Morgan's porch and sat on the top step. "I said my name is Billy," he repeated.

"Oh, you don't want to be called Pinky anymore?"

Pinky shook his head.

26

"I see," Mrs. Morgan said. "And why is that?" 2 8

"Because I don't like pink," Pinky told her. "And a boy shouldn't have a pink bike. And Pinky is a dumb name for a boy. And a boy shouldn't play with girls."

"My goodness," Mrs. Morgan said, "I had no idea there were so many rules

for boys. Imagine if you still *did* like pink and you *wanted* to be Rex's friend. How hard it would be to have to pretend to follow all those rules."

"I don't make the rules," Pinky said.

"Oh," said Mrs. Morgan. "Then who does?"

Pinky didn't have an answer for that.

"You know, Pinky, I mean Billy, when I was young I decided to follow the rules, too. Other people's rules, I mean. It was a very silly thing to do."

"Why?" Pinky asked.

"Do you remember my telling you that I used to paint pictures? Well, I loved to paint so much it was all I wanted to do. But some of the other children made fun of me. They stuck their noses in the air and called me 'the artist.' That hurt. Because as much as I loved to paint, I hated feeling different.

"So one day, I put away all my brushes and I never took them out again. I pretended I liked doing the things the other children liked to do.

"Soon they stopped making fun of me. And over time I forgot all about painting. Then the other day I was looking at that beautiful pink bush and it all came back to me. And, oh, the sadness that came with it."

Mrs. Morgan paused. "I know why that bully pushed you down," she went on. "It's hard to be different, isn't it, Billy? And have other children make fun of you. But, believe me, it's worse not to be yourself. Don't change for other people, Billy. Other people will come and go in your life. Do what's right for the one person who will always be with you — yourself."

Pinky sat for a long time, thinking. When he saw Rex come out of her house, he stood up.

"Going to play now, Billy?" Mrs. Morgan asked.

He nodded, then turned back. "I don't think I want to be called Billy," he said. "Okay?"

32

Mrs. Morgan smiled. "Okay,
Pinky. Now, run along. Your friend
is waiting." 3 ろ

Chapter 6
Nice Pink Sneakers

34

On Monday morning as they walked to school, Pinky told Rex how hard it had been to get his stuffed animals back from Amanda. "She only let me have them when I said she could keep two," he said.

"Not Pretzel, I hope," said Rex.

"No way!" Pinky replied. "Pretzel missed me the most. Even Amanda understood that."

"I'm glad you changed your mind about being called Billy." Rex could hardly believe it when Pinky had told her that part of the story.

"Me, too," said Pinky.

They had almost reached the school door when they heard a familiar voice behind them.

"Hi, girls!"

"Ignore him," Rex whispered.

Pinky turned around. Kevin was smirking at him.

"Nice pink sneakers," Kevin said.

Pinky looked the older boy in the eyes. "I like them," he said.

Kevin shrugged. "Isn't pink every girl's favorite color?" 36

"Mine's yellow," said Rex.

Pinky walked straight up to Kevin and poked him in the chest. "It's none of your business what I like," he said. "Or who I play with. I'm not a sissy and I'm not a girl. And if you think so, it just shows how dumb you are."

Kevin's mouth hung open as Pinky poked him a second time and then walked away. "Come on, Rex," he said, "let's go."

"Oh, yeah?" Kevin called after them. But Pinky noticed that the bully no longer sounded quite so tough.

Chapter 7
A Present

"A present for me?" Mrs. Morgan asked, surprised to find Pinky and Rex standing at her front door with a beautifully wrapped box.

Pinky nodded.

"But why? It's not my birthday."

"Open it!" Rex urged her neighbor.

When Mrs. Morgan saw what lay inside, she broke into a big smile.

"Paints and brushes. Oh, my."

"Now you can paint that flower bush," Pinky said.

Mrs. Morgan nodded. "That explosion of pink," she said. "Is pink still your favorite color?"

"Yes, ma'am," said Pinky.

"Then the first picture I paint will be for you." 40

Pinky didn't care much about having a picture of flowers, but he didn't say so. All that mattered was that Mrs. Morgan was happy. And for the first time in days, so was he.